# The Sneeze

SO-BCW-228

Written by Jill Eggleton
Illustrated by John Bennett

Monkey is in the jungle.

Monkey is up
in the tree.

Monkey went A-ACHOO.

4

A leaf went up
in the sky.

Parrot is in the jungle.

Parrot is up
in the tree.

Parrot went A-ACHOO.

A feather went up
in the sky.

Elephant is in the jungle.

Elephant is under
the tree.

Elephant went A-ACHOO.

Parrot went up
in the sky.

Monkey went up
in the sky, too.

# A Flow Diagram

# Guide Notes

**Title: The Sneeze**
**Stage:** Early (1) – Red

**Genre:** Fiction
**Approach:** Guided Reading
**Processes:** Thinking Critically, Exploring Language, Processing Information
**Written and Visual Focus:** Flow Diagram, Speech Bubbles, Illustrative Text

## THINKING CRITICALLY

(sample questions)
- What do you think this story could be about?
- Look at the title and read it to the children.
- What do you think made Monkey and Parrot sneeze?
- What do you think made Elephant sneeze?
- Why do you think Monkey and Parrot went up in the air when Elephant sneezed?

## EXPLORING LANGUAGE

### Terminology
Title, cover, illustrations, author, illustrator

### Vocabulary
**Interest words:** sneeze, monkey, leaf, jungle, parrot, feather, elephant
**High-frequency words:** the, is, in, too, went, under, up
**Positional words:** up, under, in

### Print Conventions
Capital letter for sentence beginnings and names (**M**onkey, **P**arrot, **E**lephant), periods, commas, exclamation marks